PUPPY DOG PALS

Walking the Bob

W9-AUQ-016

WITHDRAWN

Adapted by Victoria Saxon

**Based on the episode "Walking the Bob"
by Bob Smiley for the series created by Harland Williams**

Illustrated by Maryam Sefati

A GOLDEN BOOK • NEW YORK

ISBN 978-0-7364-3972-5 (trade) — ISBN 978-0-7364-3973-2 (ebook)
Printed in the United States of America
10 9 8 7 6 5 4 3 2 1

Rolly and **Bingo** are pugs. Bob is their person. When Rolly and Bingo talk, all Bob hears is ***Ruff! Ruff!*** Normally Bob walks the dogs, but today is different. Today Bob's doctor has given him some eye drops, so his vision will be blurry for a while. Now the dogs will have to walk Bob!

18
MON

"Bob can't see very well," Bingo says to Rolly.
"We need to help him get home."
"Cool!" says Rolly. "That can be our mission!"

Bob accidentally walks into the coat rack at the doctor's office. He thinks it's a person.

"Oops! Sorry, sir," Bob says.

Oh, boy! The puppies really need to help him.

"Come on, Bob!" says Bingo. "Follow us!"

Outside, Bob almost doesn't recognize a couple of his neighbors, Chloe and her mom.

"My puppies and I are headed home," Bob says to them, but he walks in the wrong direction!

The pugs tug on their leashes.

"Wrong way, Bob!" says Bingo.

"Our house is that way," adds Rolly.

Ruff!

Ruff!

Oh, no! Bob pulls the pugs into a park. The puppies try to guide him through the playground safely, but it's tough.

After getting Bob away from the playground,
the pups continue to try to walk him home. But
he wants to buy flowers.

"Bob, those aren't flowers," says Rolly.
"They're drumsticks," says Bingo.

Bob gives a drumstick flower to a policeman.
"A pretty flower for a pretty lady!" Bob says.

Bob even tries to give a drumstick flower to a vending machine. "Beautiful day, isn't it?" Bob says to the machine.

Ruff! Ruff!

Now Bob wants to buy fruit. He goes into a big store—and heads for the sporting-goods aisle.

"I don't know what kind of fruit this is," he says, "but it's way too hard to eat."

"That's not fruit," the dogs say. "That's a golf ball!"

Ruff! Ruff!

"Wow! This has got to be the biggest orange ever!" says Bob.

"That's not an orange," Bingo and Rolly say. "It's a basketball!"

Bingo and Rolly get an idea. They push shopping carts into Bob's path to steer him toward the fruit section.

Back outside the store,
Bob feels some drops and
thinks it's raining.

"It's not raining," says
Rolly. "Someone is watering
plants above us."

"I guess Bob can't tell
the difference," Bingo says.

Ruff! Ruff!

Ruff!
Ruff!

Bob wants to buy a rain hat. He goes into a store.
"That's the music store again, Bob!" says Bingo.
"They don't sell flowers or hats in there," Rolly adds.
"And that's not a rain hat!" they tell him when he
comes out. "It's a drum!"

Bingo and Rolly walk Bob onto a bus. Bob thinks he's still out on the sidewalk, so while the bus drives along, he keeps walking. Bingo and Rolly guide him past the other passengers . . .

. . . and right out the back door. They've made it to their neighborhood!

"I can barely see it, but I'm pretty sure that's
my house right there," says Bob.
"We did it!" shout Rolly and Bingo. "Yay!"

The next morning, Bob can see well again!

"It's Bob!" Rolly and Bingo say when Bob comes downstairs to greet them. "He's awake!"

But all Bob hears is **Ruff! Ruff!**

Ruff!   **Ruff!**